Learning with Kelsey Mac

by Kendra Williams

Learning with Kelsey Mac

ISBN: 978-1-09838-440-1

Publisher: MacDae Enterprises, LLC
Publishing

Formatted by: MacDae Enterprises, LLC
Edited by: Kendra Williams

Dedication

This simple sentence book is dedicated to my girls, Kelsey and Joelle.
We want to see more of our girls learning, creating, and exploring.
You have inspired me and this is my gift to you and all the other little black girls.
Keep learning and growing every day.

Love, Mommy

Hi my name is Kelsey.
My family calls me Kelsey Mac.

I love to learn.

Today, I am learning **five new** activities.

Will you learn with me? It will be fun.

We will learn our **ABC's** using this chart.

We will learn to count up to **ten.**
Using these number blocks.

We will learn our colors.
We will paint with different colors
to create a beautiful picture.

We will learn our shapes.
We will use a puzzle to match
the shapes.

We will learn our farm animals.
We will read a book.

We learned five new things today.

Our ABC's

Counting to **ten**

Our **colors**

Our **shapes**

Our **farm animals**

Learning is so much fun.

What will we learn next time?